The Manger Mouse

The Manger Mouse
What She Saw and Did and Got
On the Very First Christmas

Joel Wells

Illustrated by Annette Boarini Anderson

THE THOMAS MORE PRESS
Chicago, Illinois

ISBN: 0-88347-255-4

Long ago and far away a mouse
lived in a manger house.
The manger house,
which was really a small barn,
stood in a rocky field
just outside a tiny village
called Bethlehem.
It had walls made of stone
and a roof made of straw.
It had no windows at all.
It did have a doorway.
But there was no door to close.
Which meant that the wind
and the rain could blow in.
But the mouse did not care.
She liked her cozy nest.
It was high up
above the inside of the doorway,
in the space between two
stones, packed with moss.
The mouse was brown and
white and very small.
She had no name because
no one ever gave her one.
But she had very bright black
eyes that let her see everything
that went on in the manger
house.

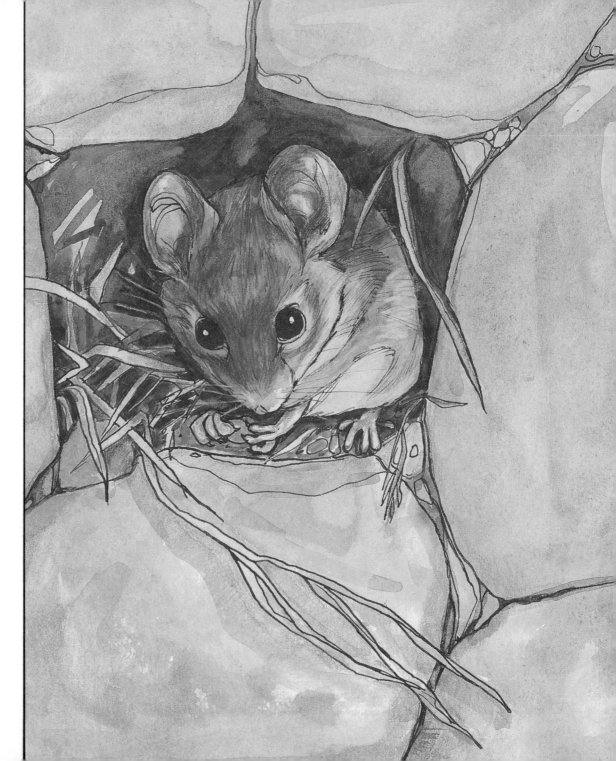

And what went on in
the manger house was this:
The cow stood
and swished its tail.
The two sheep lay down
and made themselves into
wooly balls.
The old man came in the
morning and drove the sheep
out into the rocky field.
Then he put some grain into
the manger trough
for the cow to eat.
He filled the wooden bucket
with water and went away.
Just before dark
the old woman came.
She carried a pail.
She drove the sheep
back inside.

She sat down on a little stool
beside the cow and sang,

"We milk the cow
that gives the cream
that makes the cheese we eat."

When the milk pail was full
she covered it with a cloth.
She wiped her hands
on the front of her apron.
From its pocket
she took a hunk of crusty bread
and a lump of yellow cheese
and ate them.

When she had gone
and it was quite dark
the manger mouse
climbed out of her nest.
She ran down the wall
and drank some water from the
rim of the wooden bucket.
She ate some grain
from the manger trough.

And sometimes, but not often,
she found some crumbs
of bread and cheese
that the woman had dropped.
The cheese was the best thing
the manger mouse had ever
tasted.
But there was never more than
the tiniest bit of it to be found.
She drank a few more drops
of water, then climbed back
up into her nest
where she watched and waited.
But nothing else ever happened.

UNTIL . . .
one very dark and chilly night,
long after the woman had gone
away, the manger mouse
heard noises
and saw a light.
The old man came through
the doorway carrying a lamp.
Behind him came another man,
leading a strange little donkey.
And on the donkey
rode a young woman.
Both men helped her down.
She seemed very tired,
too tired to stand.
The first man went away,
but he left the lamp.
The new man gently
pushed the cow aside.
He tied up the little donkey
behind the sheep.
He pulled fresh hay from
the corner of the manger house
and piled it high to make
a bed for the young woman.
She lay down and he
covered her with a blanket.
Then he sat down beside her,
put his head on his knees
and fell asleep.

The lamp flickered
and went out.
There was nothing more to see
so the manger mouse
wrapped her tail around her
and
ZZZZZZZzzzzzzzz.

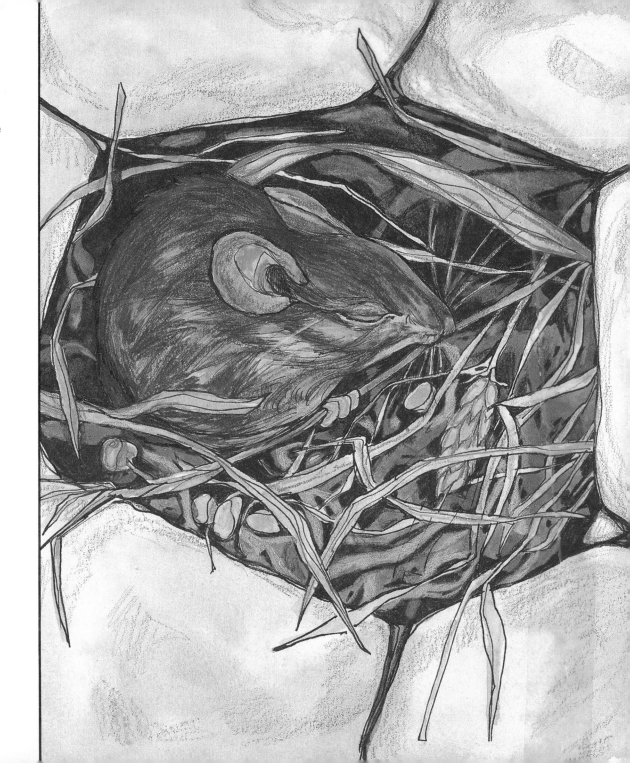

She woke with a start.
More noises, more light.
What a night! What a night!
Brightness shone in
through the doorway
But the sun had not come up.
There in the manger,
atop the straw,
swaddled in a cloth so tight,
lay a baby, newborn
and filled with life.
What a sight! What a sight!

Shouts filled the air.
Hoofbeats shook the ground.
The manger mouse peeped out
through a chink in the stones.
A great star lit the sky.
Men were running
across the field.
Driving a big flock of sheep.
When they got to the doorway
the men grew quiet.

They uncovered their heads
and knelt down on the straw,
as if this were the first
baby they ever saw.

The young woman
opened her eyes
and smiled at the shepherds.
The man picked the baby up.
He gave it to each shepherd
to hold for a moment.
Then they rose
and, silently, went away.

Morning came, and with it
the old man and woman.
The old man went about
his business as usual.
But the old woman
was very happy to see the baby.
She helped the young woman
wash the baby with a cloth she
dipped into the wooden bucket.
"What a beautiful baby boy,"
she said.
"What is his name?"
"Jesus,"
the young woman told her.
"And my name is Mary,"
she added,
"and this is my husband,
Joseph."
After the old woman left
Joseph took a loaf of bread out
of a bundle and gave half of it
to Mary.
Surely, the manger
mouse hoped,
they must have some cheese.
But they had nothing but bread
and a skin bag of water
from which they drank.

"We must get you and Jesus
to someplace warm and dry as
soon as you are able to move,
Mary," Joseph said.
Mary smiled
and told him not to worry.
"We have our animal friends
to keep us warm, Joseph."

The manger mouse did not
know how to
keep track of time.
But that night, and the next,
after Mary, Joseph and Jesus
were asleep, she climbed down
from her nest and searched for
grain and bread crumbs.
And each night she would creep
atop the manger trough to get
a closer look at the baby Jesus.
The light from the great star
poured through the doorway
and lit up his tiny face.
But he was always fast asleep.
The manger mouse was very
pleased with her new family.
She hoped that they
would never go away.
But it would be nicer still
if only they had some cheese.

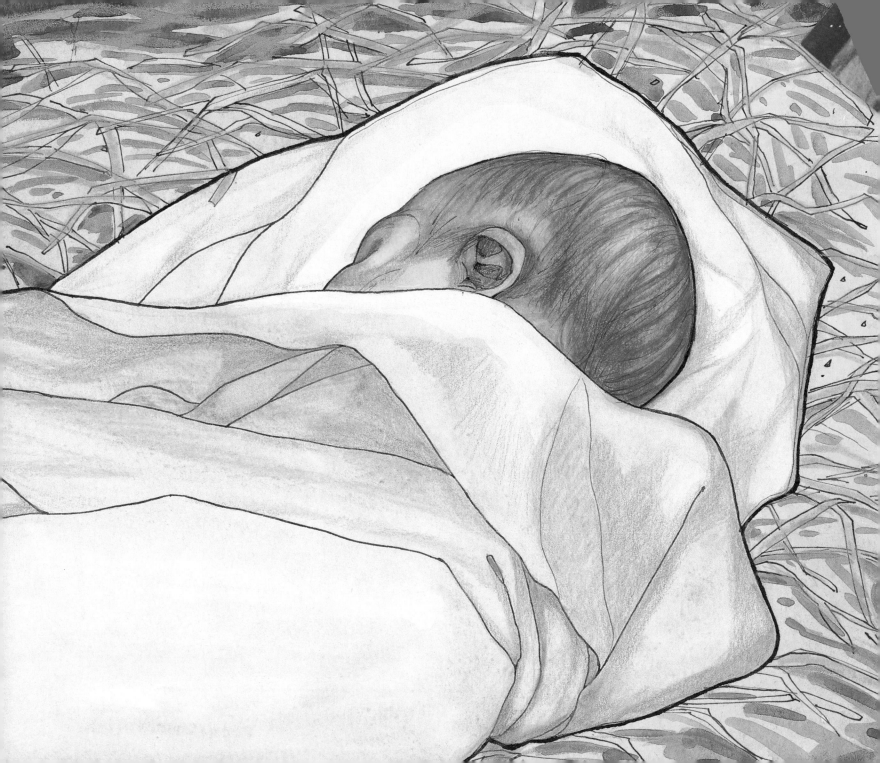

Next evening,
just as it grew dark,
the manger mouse heard
strange voices calling:

"At last! At last!"
"The star's straight above,
he must be here."

She peeped out through
the chink in the wall
and saw something
very strange, indeed.
Three men in kingly robes,
riding on great humped beasts
with long, curving necks
sat just outside the door.
One of the beasts stretched
up its head and bared huge
teeth, just a few
inches from the mouse's sight.

What a fright! What a fright!

The beasts knelt down
and the three got off.
Joseph greeted them and
invited them in.
They bowed low to Mary,
and lower still before Jesus.

From under their long capes
they drew presents
that glittered with gold.
They opened jeweled boxes
to show rich spices.
Strange and wonderful smells
filled the night air.
All these gifts they left at
the foot of the manger.

Then bowing again they
backed away outside.
They climbed back on the
strange beasts and rode
off into the starlight.

Joseph gathered up the gifts
and blew out the light.
Everyone settled in
for the night.
When all was still,
down crept the mouse.
After she had eaten her fill
and was about to climb
atop the manger, she saw
one of the baby's pink feet
peeking out of
the swaddling cloth.
This would not do!
The night was too cold.
Ever so gently the mouse
took an edge of the cloth
in her teeth.
She tugged and she folded
until the foot
was once again snug.
Then she climbed up to see
the sleeping baby's face.

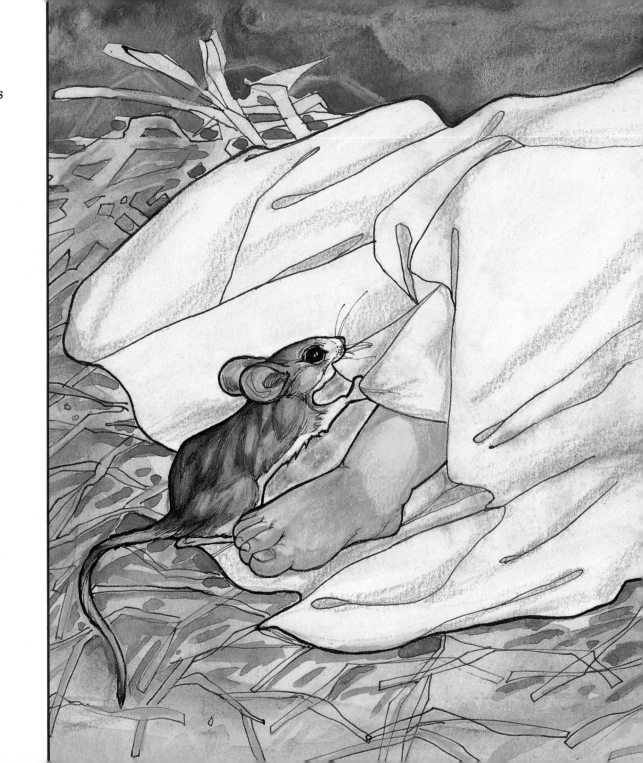

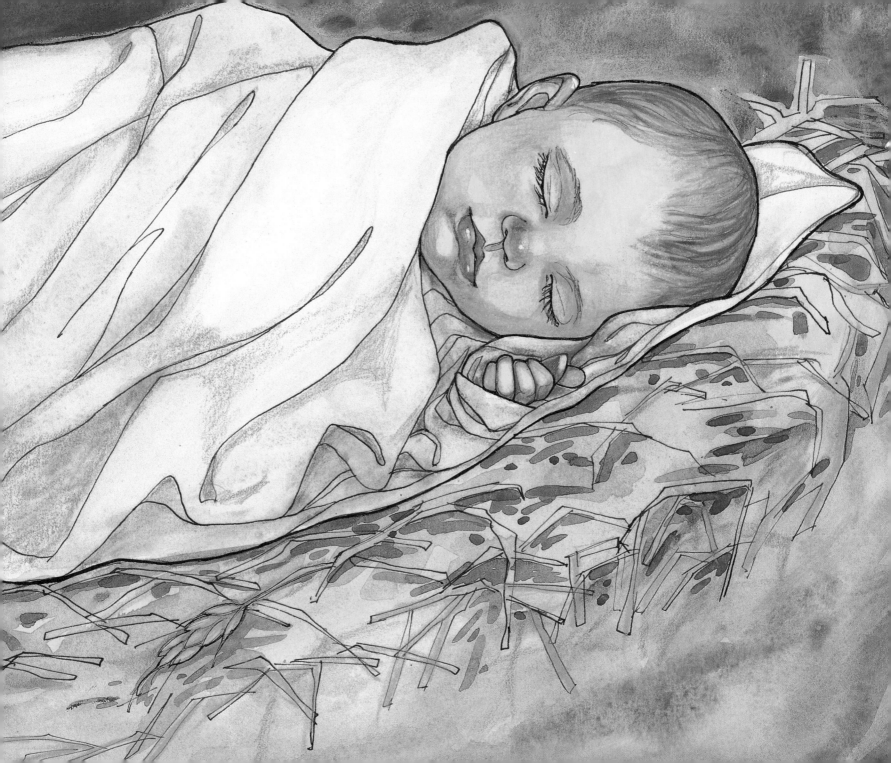

All was well . . . but wait!
Jesus opened his eyes
and looked straight
at the mouse.
And that's not all.
His mouth curled up,
his eyes did a dance,
and he gave the mouse
—there was no doubt about it
—a smile, big and wide.

Which gave the mouse such
a start that she ran back
to her nest to hide.

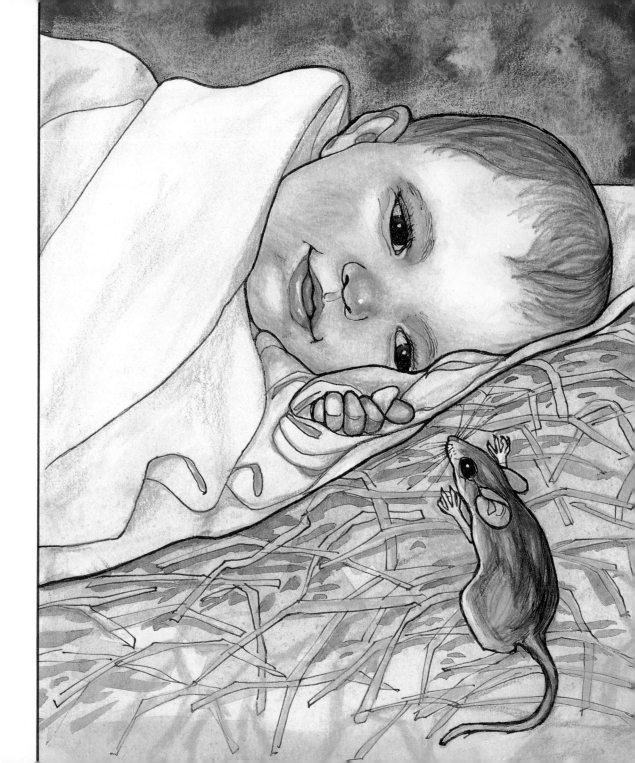

After a bit
she fell sound asleep.
She slept and she slept.
When she awoke
the sun was high in the sky.
She peeped down
through the moss.
No Mary!
No Joseph!
No baby Jesus!
All gone away.
What a loss! What a loss!

The empty manger
was all that was there.
But look!
What is that?
The manger was not really
bare. There on the straw,
where the baby had lain,
was a bright chunk of cheese,
a gift for a mouse
who had thought to be kind.

What a find! What a find!